D0239596

CROC

GOES TO THE DENTIST

Written by Sue Graves
Illustrated by David Parkins

W
FRANKLIN WATTS
LONDON·SYDNEY

Croc didn't always look after her teeth. She didn't always clean her teeth **in the morning**.

She didn't always clean her teeth **at night**.

She said she was **too busy**, **too tired**...
or **she forgot**!

Croc liked to eat **lots of sweets**.
She liked **fizzy drinks**, too.
Her friends said they were **not good for her teeth**.

But Croc liked them, and she **didn't want to stop** having them.

One day, Mum told Croc that she was going to the dentist for a **check-up**. Mum said it **was important** to have check-ups at the dentist to keep your teeth healthy.

MONDAY

9.00 Swim
10.00 Float
11.00 Wash
12.00 DENTIST
1.00 Swim
2.00 Nap

Croc **was worried**. She didn't want to go to the dentist at all.

Croc went to find Dad. He was in his potting shed.
Croc told Dad about her check-up at the dentist.
She told him she **didn't want to go**.
She said the dentist might be **cross** with her
for not looking after her teeth properly.

Dad said when he was little he once got a big
toffee stuck on his tooth. His mum said he had to
go to the dentist. But he **didn't want to go**.

He **was worried** the dentist would hurt his tooth.
He was worried the dentist would be **cross**
with him for eating toffees!

But the dentist wasn't cross. He was **very kind**.
He got the toffee off Dad's tooth. It **didn't hurt**
at all. Dad said dentists **help everyone** to look
after their teeth. Croc felt a bit better.

That afternoon, Mum took Croc to see Mr Bird, the dentist. He was very kind. He let Croc ride **up and down** in the big chair.

He let her **lie down** and **sit up** in it, too.
Croc said it was **good fun!**

Then Mr Bird looked in Croc's mouth with a mirror. He let Croc look at all her teeth. He **counted** them while Croc watched.

Croc liked that. She didn't know she had
so many teeth!

Mr Bird said Croc only had **baby teeth** at the moment. He said they would soon go to make room for her **adult teeth**. He said it was important to look after the baby teeth so that the adult teeth would be **strong and healthy**.

Mr Bird said Croc's teeth needed a **really good clean**. He said it was **important** to keep teeth clean and healthy. Mr Bird cleaned Croc's teeth carefully. It didn't hurt at all. Soon Croc's teeth were **sparkling**.

Then Mr Bird showed Croc what she should eat.

He said it was important to **eat healthy food**.

He said to try to have any sweets and fizzy drinks

at **meal times**... and only as **a treat**.

He said lots of sugar is not good for teeth.

Before she went home, Mr Bird gave Croc
a new toothbrush. It looked like a big banana!
Croc said it was the **best toothbrush** ever.
She said she would brush **every morning**
and **every night**.

24

Mr Bird said that was a very good idea.

After that, Croc **remembered** to clean her teeth carefully every morning and every night.

She **remembered** to choose drinks and foods that weren't sweet or sticky.

Soon Croc had very clean, healthy teeth.
Everyone said they **sparkled**!

A note about sharing this book

The *Experiences Matter* series has been developed to provide a starting point for further discussion on how children might deal with new experiences. It provides opportunities to explore ways of developing coping strategies as they face new challenges.
The series is set in the jungle with animal characters reflecting typical behaviour traits and attitudes often seen in young children.

Croc Goes to the Dentist
This story looks at some of the typical concerns a child might have when visiting the dentist for the first time. It aims to allay any fears the child might have but also takes the opportunity to highlight the importance of good hygiene and a healthy diet when caring for their teeth.

How to use the book
The book is designed for adults to share with either an individual child, or a group of children, and as a starting point for discussion.

The book also provides visual support and repeated words and phrases to build reading confidence.

Before reading the story
Choose a time to read when you and the children are relaxed and have time to share the story.

Spend time looking at the illustrations and talk about what the book might be about before reading it together.

Encourage children to employ a phonics first approach to tackling new words by sounding the words out.

After reading, talk about the book with the children:

- Look through the pictures in the book and ask the children to discuss what it might be about before reading the story.

- After reading the book together, ask the children to retell the story in their own words.

- Invite the children to share their own experiences of going to the dentist. What was it like? Was the dentist kind? What did the dentist do? Did the child get a sticker, toothbrush or toothpaste?

Remind the children to listen carefully while others speak and to wait for their turn.

- Find out how many children clean their teeth both morning and evening. Why do they think this is important?

- Talk about the importance of a good diet to maintain healthy teeth. Why do the children think sweets, sticky foods and sugary drinks should only be eaten or drunk at mealtimes and then only as a special treat?

- Invite the children to help you make a wall chart of healthy foods that are good for teeth. They may either draw pictures of the foods or cut them out of magazines to make a collage. When finished, display the chart as a future reference point.

For Isabelle, William A, William G, George, Max, Emily,

Leo, Caspar, Felix, Tabitha, Phoebe, Harry and Libby – S.G.

This edition published in 2023 by
Hodder & Stoughton

Copyright © Hodder & Stoughton, 2023
All rights reserved

The right of Hodder & Stoughton to be identified as the author
of this Work has been asserted by them in accordance with the
Copyright, Designs and Patents Act 1988.

Published by Hachette
Children's Group
Part of Hodder & Stoughton

A CIP catalogue record for this book is available
from the British Library

ISBN 978 1 444 97333 7 (Hardback)
ISBN 978 1 444 97335 1 (Paperback)

Printed in China

Hodder Children's Group
An imprint of Hachette Children's Group

www.hachettechildrens.co.uk